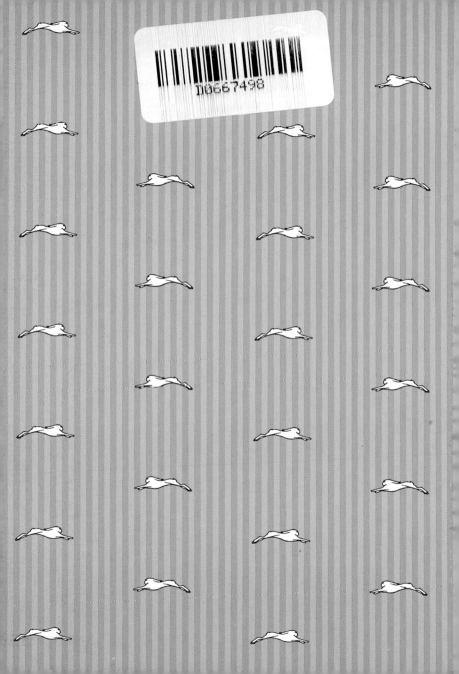

PICTURE CREDITS

COVER
Frank S. Guild, 1903

TITLE PAGE
Anonymous, 1900's

TABLE OF CONTENTS
Anonymous, 1880's

BACK COVER
F. Y. Cory, 1924

ISBN 0–8118–0185–3

Library of Congress Cataloging in Publication Data available.

Distributed in Canada by Raincoast Books,
112 East Third Avenue, Vancouver, B.C. V5T 1C8

10 9 8 7 6 5 4 3 2

Chronicle Books
275 Fifth Street
San Francisco, California 94103

Acknowledgments
We thank the following for permission to use these
poems: Harper and Brothers for "What Is It", by Marie
Louise Allen, from *A Pocketful of Rhymes,* copyright 1939.
Viking for "Rabbits", by Zhenya Gay, from *Jingle Jangle,*
copyright 1953. Macmillan for "Listen Rabbit", by Aileen
Fisher, from *Listen Rabbit,* copyright 1964. The Literary
Trustees of Walter de la Mare and the Society of Authors for
"The Hare". Atheneum for "When", by Brian Swann, from
To See the World Afresh, copyright 1974. Harcourt, Brace,
Jovanovich for "Song of the Rabbits Outside the Tavern", by
Elizabeth Coatsworth, from *Rainbow in the Sky,* copyright
1941. Macmillan for "Rabbits", by Dorothy W. Baruch,
from *Under Tent of the Sky,* copyright 1937.

A Classic Illustrated Treasury

RABBITS

CHRONICLE BOOKS • SAN FRANCISCO

Table of Contents

−*Albrecht Dürer, 1502*

THE HARE

In the black furrow of a field
I saw an old witch-hare this night;
And she cocked a lissome ear,
And she eyed the moon so bright,
And she nibbled of the green;
And I whispered "Whsst! witch-hare,"
Away like a ghostie o'er the field
She fled, and left the moonlight there.

—*Walter de la Mare*

—Edwin Noble, 1909

ALL THINGS THAT LOVE THE SUN

All things that love the sun are out of doors;
The sky rejoices in the morning's birth;
The grass is bright with rain-drops;—on the moors
The hare is running races in her mirth;
And with her feet she from the plashy earth
Raises a mist, that glittering in the sun,
Runs with her all the way, wherever she doth run.

—William Wordsworth

THE NAMES OF RABBIT

The wall-eyed one, the looker to the side,
And also the hedge-frisker,
The stag of the stubble, long-eared
The animal of the stubble, the springer,
The wild animal, the jumper,
The short animal, the lurker,
The swift-as-wind, the skulker,
The shagger, the squatter in the hedge,
The dew-beater, the dew hopper,
The sitter on its form, the hopper in the grass,
The fidgety-footed one, the sitter on the ground,
The light-foot, the sitter in the bracken,
The stag of the cabbages, the cropper of herbage,
The low creeper, the sitter-still,
The small-tailed one, the one who turns to the hills.

—Anonymous

—Pamela Bianco, 1925

−*Noël Hopking, 1944*

WHAT IS IT?

Tall ears,
Twinkly nose,
Tiny tail,
And – hop, he goes!

What *is* he –
Can you guess?
I feed him carrots
And watercress.

His ears are long,
His tail is small –
And he doesn't make any
Noise at all!

Tall ears,
Twinkly nose,
Tiny tail,
And – hop, he goes!

– Marie Louise Allen

MEETING THE EASTER BUNNY

On Easter morn at early dawn
   before the cocks were crowing,
I met a bob-tail bunnykin
   and asked where he was going,
" 'Tis in the house and out the house
   a-tipsy, tipsy-toeing,
'Tis round the house and 'bout the
house
   a-lightly I am going."
"But what is that of every hue
   you carry in your basket?
" 'Tis eggs of gold and eggs of blue;
   I wonder that you ask it.
'Tis chocolate eggs and bonbon eggs
   and eggs of red and gray,
For every child in every house
   on bonny Easter Day."
He perked his ears and winked his eye
   and twitched his little nose;
He shook his tail—what tail he had—
   and stood up on his toes.
"I must be gone before the sun;
   the East is growing gray;
'Tis almost time for bells to chime."
   So he hippety-hopped away.

                       —*Rowena Bastin Bennett*

—Anonymous, 1900's

RABBIT EARS

A rabbit's ears are made of plush
And lined with lovely pink;
They tell him when he ought to rush,
Or when to stop and think.

–May Carlton Lord

–Anonymous, 1900's

–Harriet M. Bennett, 1891

RABBITS

All kinds of rabbits
Have different habits:
The little ones jump,
The big ones go thump.

–Zhenya Gay

THE RABBIT

When they said the time to hide was mine,
I hid back under the thick grape vine.

And while I was still for the time to pass,
A little gray thing came out of the grass.

He hopped his way through the melon bed
And sat down close by a cabbage head.

He sat down close where I could see,
And his big still eyes looked hard at me,

His big eyes bursting out of the rim,
And I looked back very hard at him.

–Elizabeth Madox Roberts

—Japanese screen, Kano School

from LISTEN RABBIT

On the way home
I thought about ears . . .
the hundreds of things
a cottontail hears
probably,
possibly,
liker than not
that *we* never know
are Whether or What:

Sound of spiders taking a walk,
sound of aphids sucking a stalk,
sound of beetles dodging a hawk,
sound of fireflies talking their talk.

—Aileen Fisher

—Edwin Noble, 1909

from A MAKE-BELIEVE

All is welcome to my crunching,
  Finding, grinding,
  Milling, munching,
  Gobbling, lunching,
Fore-toothed, three-lipped mouth –
Eating side way, round way, flat way,
Eating this way, eating that way,
Every way at once!

–George MacDonald

WHEN

When I'm on your lawn
you all go quiet
hoping to catch me

I am listening
though still

When you get too close
I take off
stretching myself out
to twice my length

Don't follow or
if you do

prepare to shrink
and tumble to strange dark

–Brian Swann

–Anonymous, 1880's

—Anonymous, 1890's

SONG OF THE RABBITS
OUTSIDE THE TAVERN

We who play under the pines,
We who dance in the snow
That shines blue in the light of the moon
Sometimes halt as we go,
Stand with our ears erect,
Our noses testing the air,
To gaze at the golden world
Behind the windows there.

Suns they have in a cave
And stars each on a tall white stem,
And the thought of fox or night owl
Seems never to trouble them,
They laugh and eat and are warm,
Their food seems ready at hand,
While hungry out in the cold
We little rabbits stand.

–K. F. Edmund von Freyhold, 1920's

But they never dance as we dance,
They have not the speed nor the grace.
We scorn both the cat and the dog
Who lie by their fireplace.
We scorn them licking their paws,
Their eyes on an upraised spoon,
We who dance hungry and wild
Under a winter's moon.

–Elizabeth Coatsworth

FINGER PLAY

This little bunny said, "Let's play."
This little bunny said, "In the hay."
This one saw a man with a gun.
This one said, "This isn't fun."
This one said, "I'm off for a run."
Bang! went the gun,
They ran away
And didn't come back for a year and a day.

                                        –Anonymous

–Anonymous, 1890's

−Charles Collins, 1880's

A GOOD REASON

"Why do you wear your tail so short?"
   The kittens asked the rabbit.
"I think the reason," he replied,
   "Is simply force of habit."

−Caroline M. Fuller

RABBITS

My two white rabbits
Chase each other
With humping, bumping backs
  They go hopping, hopping,
  And their long ears
    Go flopping, flopping.
      And they
      Make faces
      With their noses
      Up and down.

And in one corner
Under a loose bush
I saw something shivering the leaves.
And I pushed
And looked.
And I found–
There
In a hole
In the ground–
Three baby rabbits
Hidden away.
      And *they*
      Made faces
      With their noses
      Up and down.

–Dorothy W. Baruch

−H. Allingham, 1909

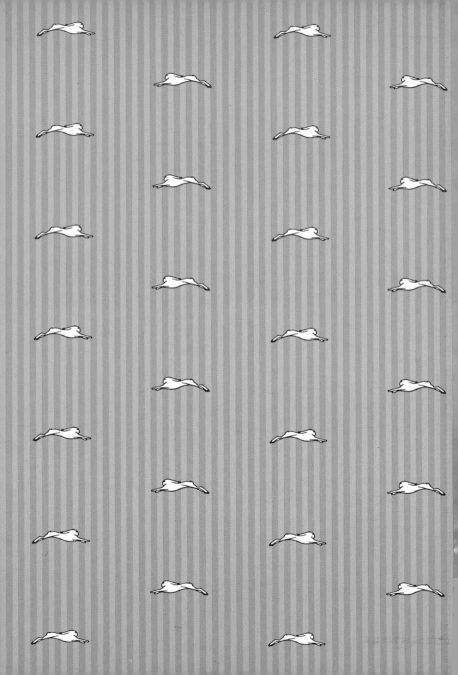